THE DALLAS TITANS
Get Ready for Bed

A CHARLOTTE ZOLOTOW BOOK

THE DALLAS TITANS
Get Ready for Bed

By Karla Kuskin

Illustrations by Marc Simont

Harper & Row, Publishers

The Dallas Titans Get Ready for Bed
Text copyright © 1986 by Karla Kuskin
Illustrations copyright © 1986 by Marc Simont
Printed in the U.S.A. All rights reserved.
Designed by Trish Parcell
10 9 8 7 6 5 4 3 2 1
First Edition

Library of Congress Cataloging-in-Publication Data
Kuskin, Karla.
    The Dallas Titans get ready for bed.

    "A Charlotte Zolotow book."
    Summary: Follows a fictitious football team off the
field, into the locker room, and to their homes,
describing the normal routine after a game and examining
the uniforms and pieces of equipment as they are
removed.
    1. Football—Equipment and supplies—Juvenile
literature.   2. Football—Uniforms—Juvenile literature.
[1. Football]   I. Simont, Marc, ill.   II. Title.
GV959.K87 1986   796.332′028   83-49470
ISBN 0-06-023562-4
ISBN 0-06-023563-2 (lib. bdg.)

The big game is over. Under the lights the football field shines green. Above the green field the high night sky is full of yells and screams, cheers and stars. It is twenty-seven minutes after ten o'clock on Monday night, and the Dallas Titans have just won a big game. The cheerleaders do double-reverse banana splits and we-are-roaring, we-are-scoring slips and slides. The crowd keeps going crazy.

The players jog off the field laughing and slapping each other's backs. Four men carry Blimp on their shoulders. Blimp is number seventeen. He made the winning touchdown. Up in the stands Blimp's mother, Mrs. Blimp, cries because she is so happy.

Three men carry Jones. Jones is number twelve. He is the quarterback. Jones threw the winning pass to Blimp. Jones's sister hugs Blimp's mother. More laughing and crying. If the fans were balloons they would burst.

It looks as if everybody in the world is in the locker room. There are forty-five players, eight coaches, a doctor for bones, and a doctor for everything else. The equipment man is there, the trainer is checking bruises, his assistants are handing out towels and ice bags.

The owner is smiling. There are reporters taking notes for magazines and newspapers, photographers firing flashbulbs, a TV cameraman, and Zelinka's little brother. Zelinka's knees hurt. He is sitting on a bench, with an ice bag on each knee.

During the game all the Titans wear hard, heavy helmets to protect their heads. The helmets are held on by chin straps. As the players run off the field they unfasten the chin straps. They throw them in the air. Fans catch them. Straps land on the grass, in the stands, and on the floor of the locker room.

The helmets are white with a green stripe running down the middle and three green diamonds on each side. Each helmet has a face guard—some of them have many bars across the face; some of them have a few. Blimp's face mask looks like a birdcage. Jones just has one bar in front of his mouth. He needs to see clearly when he throws the ball.

Twenty-four players wear plastic mouth guards attached to their face masks. They spit them out. Trample whistles through the space left by his missing teeth.

The owner is still smiling. She is standing on a
bench in the locker room. She says, "Congratula-
tions. Tonight you won a big game." Loud cheers.
The owner says, "The game you play next Sunday
will be even bigger. When you win that one we will
have a tremendous party." The Titans stamp their
feet. Louder cheers.

The head coach gets up. He is Coach Dutch Scorch. He does not smile. He never does. His voice is loud. It always is. He says, "O.K., guys, into the showers." He says, "Next Sunday is the big game so we have to work hard all week. Tomorrow morning at nine I want everybody on the field for practice. Now out of your uniforms, into the showers, and home to bed." No cheers.

Jones says, "Rats."

Bones says, "It isn't fair." He kicks the door to his locker.

"It's still early," says Trample. "I don't want to go to bed."

Zelinka tries to pull his shirt off. He has so much padding on he can hardly move. Bones helps him. All over the locker room players help the players next to them pull off their shirts. These are called football jerseys. The Titans' football jerseys are white with green stripes. Each player has his number on the front and his name *and* his number on the back.

The players are very wet with sweat, and muddy. Forty-three men throw their jerseys on the floor. Thudd and Mower are neat. They drop their jerseys in a big laundry bin.

The players who get pushed the most and do the most pushing out on the field wear the most padding under their uniforms. The padding is to protect them against thumping and bumping, mauling and falling. Mudd, Mower, and Trample unlace their enormous shoulder pads and take them off.

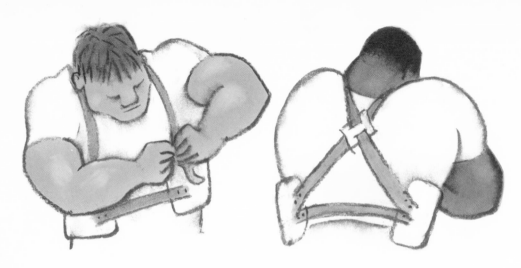

They wear rib pads too. These are like vests made of hard rubber covered with foam rubber. Some men wear smaller shoulder pads. Some do not wear rib pads. The less padding a player wears, the easier it is for him to run fast. There are rib and shoulder pads lying everywhere, hanging everywhere, falling everywhere in the crowded locker room.

Sixteen linemen have their arms taped. This makes their arms stronger so they can block and push better. Each man cuts through the sticky tape with a sharp tool. There is a layer of soft material under the tape.

There is soft material and tape on the benches and the floor. Elbow pads and wrist pads come off. And gloves. Ten men wear silky gloves. These make it easier to hold on to the ball with sweaty hands. Four of them wear just one glove. Twelve of the gloves land on the floor. One flies into a laundry bin. Three are lost forever.

The Titans wear cutoff T-shirts under their padding. This keeps the pads from rubbing their skin. Mower and Thudd put their T-shirts into the laundry bin. Neatly. The other forty-three T-shirts are strewn around the locker room. Strewn means they are lying all over the place.

Shoes come off next. They are called cleats. Eleven men taped their cleats on so they could not come loose during the game. Now they cut the tape, remove the shoes, and wiggle their toes. When the game began tonight, the cleats were white leather. Now they are the color of mud, and the soles are studded with mud between the studs. The studs are hard, black rubber bumps on the soles of the cleats. They help keep a player from slipping.

Punt and Wallup are kickers. Kickers only play when it is time to kick. Wallup wears special shoes that are half black and half white. Punt kicks barefoot. He kicks with the side of his foot, the way a soccer player does.

The Titans take their pants off. The pants are white with green stripes running down the outside of each leg. The stripes and pants end at the knee. The pants lace in front and have a belt. There is plenty of padding between a player and his pants. There are hip pads around the waist and hips, thigh pads that fit in pockets inside the pants, and knee pads shaped like horseshoes. Under his pants, each man wears a jockstrap. There is a plastic, protective cup inside that.

Thudd has a sore back. He cannot bend to get his socks off. One of the trainer's assistants helps him. Thudd wears two pairs of socks. Most players do. First they put on short white socks, and over those they wear uniform socks. These do not have heels or toes. They are knee-high and have two green stripes around the tops. Jones, Bones, Zetz, and

Scramble wear four pairs of socks each. There are
twelve men who wear three pairs each. After all the
socks have been taken off, there are one hundred
and ninety-eight socks on the locker-room floor.
There are thirteen socks in a laundry bin, six on top
of Zelinka's locker, and three in a wastebasket.

When all the players have taken off their shirts and pants, socks and shoes, shoulder, rib, hip, thigh, and knee pads; when arms and elbows have been checked and seventy-seven sprains and bruises have been treated in eighty-nine ways; everybody takes a shower.

Standing on the field in their uniforms and padding, the Titans look like giants or bulldozers.

Standing in the showers without their uniforms and padding, they look like small wet whales. Blimp sings in the shower. He sings a song his mother once taught him about a duck. Bomberg yells because he has soap in his eyes. Zelinka throws him a towel.

By now the floor of the locker room has totally
disappeared. It is covered with towels and socks;
pads, socks, and tape; socks, shirts, and jerseys;
wristbands, gloves, socks, shoes, and underwear.

Jones cannot find his left loafer. Coach Scorch
cannot find his lucky hat. Zelinka cannot find his
little brother.

After the Titans have showered they put on street clothes. Twenty-eight men get into brown, striped, green, gray, and plaid pants. Seventeen wear jeans. They slip on sport shirts, T-shirts, six sweaters, and thirteen sweatshirts. Eight men wear sport jackets, twelve wear windbreakers, and five put on jean jackets. Trample buttons up the new cardigan his grandmother knitted for him.

The Titans go home. Nineteen of them have sandwiches. Twenty-five have more than that. Bones is not hungry. He wants to watch a late movie, but Coach Scorch would be angry if he did. It is time to go to bed.

The Titans put on their pajamas. Thirty-three just wear the bottoms. Thudd wears a nightshirt.

The stars flicker. The moon grows pale. The Titans sleep. Forty-three snore. Zetz mumbles. Trample whistles through the space where his teeth are missing.

The Titans sleep like tops. They sleep like logs.
They sleep like babies. And as they sleep they
dream. They dream about miles of tape and

padding. They dream about running and winning forever. They dream about socks and Sunday afternoon. Sunday afternoon, that's the big game.